Also by Mark Powers

The **SPY TOYS** series

Illustrated by Tim Wesson

Spy Toys
Spy Toys: Out of Control!
Spy Toys: Undercover

SPACE DETECTIVES

MARK POWERS

Illustrated by
DAPO ADEOLA

BLOOMSBURY
CHILDREN'S BOOKS
LONDON   OXFORD   NEW YORK   NEW DELHI   SYDNEY

BLOOMSBURY CHILDREN'S BOOKS
Bloomsbury Publishing Plc
50 Bedford Square, London WC1B 3DP, UK
29 Earlsfort Terrace, Dublin 2, Ireland

BLOOMSBURY, BLOOMSBURY CHILDREN'S BOOKS and the Diana logo
are trademarks of Bloomsbury Publishing Plc

First published in Great Britain in 2021 by Bloomsbury Publishing Plc

A catalogue record for this book is available from the British Library

ISBN: PB: 978-1-5266-0318-0; eBook: 978-1-5266-0316-6

4 6 8 10 9 7 5 3

Printed and bound in Great Britain by CPI Group (UK) Ltd, Croydon CR0 4YY

To find out more about our authors and books visit www.bloomsbury.com
and sign up for our newsletters

For Richard Lee

With thanks to Jo, Kate, Zöe, Lucy,
Emily, Namra, Jessica and Jet

– Mark

To the memory of my good friend
Glen, the most out-of-this-world
person I know

– Dapo

PROLOGUE

The lone figure stared at the laptop screen and gave a chuckle.

In the darkened room, it was impossible to tell whether the figure was young or old, male or female, human or alien. But there was no mistaking the pure evil in its laugh.

The task that lay ahead was difficult. A few details remained to be checked. But if the plan succeeded, the result would be unimaginable terror ...

A muffled voice called, interrupting the figure's thoughts. The figure closed the laptop and went downstairs for dinner. It was fish fingers.

Chapter 1

Welcome to
Starville

It was another perfect day on Starville – the most astonishing place in the galaxy. A gigantic space station, Starville sailed silently overhead in orbit around the Earth and was home to over a million humans and aliens. It was a single, vast city brimming with skyscrapers, lush green parks and even a sparkling artificial sea, all enclosed by a huge and incredibly strong glass dome. Seen through a telescope from the world below, it looked like a gleaming snow globe gliding majestically through the night sky.

At the edge of a wide, tree-lined square near the centre of Starville's fanciest shopping district, two ten-year-old human boys stood behind an ice cream stall. One was tall, gawky and looked a bit like an ostrich wearing glasses. His name was Connor. The other was short, squat and constantly bristling with energy like a terrier. This was Ethan.

The square was full of humans and aliens enjoying the sunshine. Business at the ice cream stall was brisk.

'Wow,' said Ethan as he watched their latest customers, a family of tall, two-legged, blue-skinned, cow-like creatures, walk away licking their lips. 'Those Neptunian Cow People really love our Extra Minty Grapefruit and Smoky Bacon flavour! That's the fifth lot we've sold to them today.'

Connor adjusted his glasses, a sure sign there was something on his mind. 'Actually, Ethan, the Cow People are from *Pluto*, not Neptune. You should try to remember that. We wouldn't want to offend any of our customers.'

Ethan had to laugh. 'Give me a chance, mate! We've only been on Starville a week. I haven't learned all the alien races who live here yet.'

'Well, you could have memorised them all on the rocket trip up here, like I did,' said Connor. 'What were you doing?'

Ethan shrugged. 'Looking out of the

window and going, **"Blimey, I'm on a flipping rocket!"**

That and eating the cakes my mum baked for the trip. You can't learn everything in books, you know. Sometimes you need to just look around you. Or taste around you.' He scooped a stray blob of ice cream from the machine's dispenser nozzle with the end of his finger and popped it in his mouth.

Connor glared at him. 'For the last time, stop doing that. It's unhygienic. You'll get us closed down.'

'Oh yeah,' said Ethan. 'Sorry.'

'Anyway, I'd recommend getting to know all the different alien races now we're here,' said Connor. 'It might be handy for a case.'

'A case!' said Ethan, staring off into the distance. 'That's what we need!'

'Tell me about it,' grumbled Connor, folding his arms. 'I hardly think standing around all day selling ice cream is a good use of our skills.'

These boys were more than just ice cream sellers. They were **detectives**! Back home on Earth, Connor and Ethan had solved many mysteries together in their spare time, such as finding their head teacher's missing antique letter opener (long story short: magpie). As a result, the two boys had got rather good at finding the solutions to people's thorny problems. So when Ethan's Uncle Nick had invited them to spend the long summer holidays working on his ice cream stall on Starville, the pair had accepted instantly. This was their chance to be **_Space Detectives_**!

The only problem was that, so far, there didn't seem to be any mysteries on Starville to solve. Neither the impressive Space Detectives website they had created nor the adverts they posted online had brought them a single case. Well, that wasn't quite true. There had been the Case of the Stolen Priceless Fob Watch. But unfortunately this had turned very quickly into the Case of the Priceless Fob Watch That Someone Thought Was Stolen But Which Turned Out After Only Five Minutes of Looking Simply to Be in the Pocket of Their Other

Waistcoat, so there wasn't really much of a mystery to solve there. Was there no one aboard this space station who needed their help?

'One scoop of Triple Choc in a sugar-frosted waffle cone, please!' said a bright voice.

Roused from their daydream, the boys found they had a new customer. She was a human girl of about their age with two short pigtails, a T-shirt with an animated image of a cat on it, and a very expensive-looking striped bag slung over one shoulder.

'Sure thing,' said Ethan, and pressed the button on the ice cream machine labelled Triple Choc.

Fffffffzzzzssssssplatttttt!

A jet of liquid ice cream sprayed from its nozzle straight into Ethan's face.

Bleeugh!!!

'Connor? Something's up with this thing! Uncle Nick will go barmy if we've broken his ice cream machine.'

Connor rolled his eyes at their customer. 'Excuse my friend. He isn't the most technical person in the world.' He swiftly examined a small touchscreen on the ice cream machine, adjusted a setting and pressed the button.

Fffffffzzzzssssssplatttttt!

He too received a jet of liquid ice cream in the face.

Connor removed his glasses and wiped the lenses on his shirt. 'Ah. Obviously some kind of malfunction.'

'Excuse my friend,' said Ethan. 'Turns out he isn't the most technical person in the world either.' He winked at Connor, who gave him a sheepish grin.

The girl leaned over the counter to

examine the touchscreen. 'Do you mind? I know a little about computers.'

'Be our guest,' said Ethan, waggling his head to dislodge ice cream from his ears.

Swiftly, the girl's fingers danced over the touchscreen. 'Ah, *of course*,' she said. 'Your ice cream machine has the Misty 54 virus. It's a new one. Quite nasty.'

'A virus?' asked Ethan. 'So that's why it sprayed that stuff all over us? It sneezed?'

Connor shook his head. 'She means a *computer* virus. A rogue computer program that gets into people's devices and stops them working properly.'

'Fortunately for you,' said the girl, 'programming is my hobby and I'm a bit of an expert when it comes to computer viruses.' Once again her fingers tripped lightly over the touchscreen. There was a pleasing electronic jingle and a message appeared saying, **Misty 54 virus erased. All systems working normally.** 'Try it now.'

Ethan pushed the Triple Choc button again and the machine dispensed one perfect scoop of Triple Choc ice cream in a sugar-frosted waffle cone. He handed it to the girl. 'Here you go! No charge!'

'My pleasure,' said the girl, and, with a friendly wave, she sauntered away.

Connor nudged Ethan in the ribs. 'How

are we supposed to make any money if you're just going to give the ice cream away?'

'You may be a genius in lots of ways,' said Ethan, 'but trust me when it comes to understanding people. A free ice cream is a *nice* way to thank her for fixing our machine. And she's probably going to tell all her friends how great we are, and then they'll flock here and buy bucketloads of ice cream.'

Connor adjusted his glasses. 'Hmmm. We'll see.'

Suddenly, an ear-splitting roar filled the air, followed by a terrified scream.

'What the heck was that?' asked Connor, startled.

Ethan gasped and pointed at something over Connor's shoulder. 'That, mate,' he said, 'is the sound of someone calling for the Space Detectives. Come on!'

Chapter 2

No walk
in the park

The thing that Ethan was pointing at was
purple and slimy and had many nasty
sharp teeth. It looked a bit like a cross
between a slug and a pineapple – and it
was snarling angrily at the girl who had
just left their stall. It was also, Ethan
noticed, wearing a very small cowboy hat
covered with sparkling sequins, which
struck him as an odd clothing choice
for a purple slimy monster. Still, what
did he know about alien headwear
fashions?

With a greasy, crab-like claw, the creature snatched the striped bag from the girl's shoulder, snapping the strap.

'Hey!' cried the girl.

'Now listen up, pal,' announced Ethan, nimbly putting himself between the creature and the girl. 'We saw what you did. Give the bag back now and we won't call the police.'

Somewhat less nimbly, Connor arrived a moment later, panting. 'Come on now,' he said to it in a matter-of-fact voice. 'Stop messing about. That bag doesn't belong to you so do the decent thing and hand it over, eh?'

In response, the slimy purple creature opened its enormous fang-filled mouth and roared ferociously, showering him with gloopy purple spit.

Connor stood frozen, the horrid purple gunk dripping from the end of his nose. Out of the corner of his mouth he whispered to Ethan, 'I think we may be in trouble.'

The creature roared again, this time showering Ethan in its foul spit, and began to slither away down the street at tremendous speed, the girl's bag still clutched in its claw.

The girl heaved a sigh. 'Oh well. Thanks for trying to help, guys. It was ...'

Her voice suddenly trailed away as Connor and Ethan dashed to their ice cream stall and hopped aboard the shabby-looking hover-scooter parked behind it.

Ethan twisted the throttle and the hover-scooter leaped into the air with a loud chugging sound. There was a puff of smoke and off it rumbled in pursuit of the creature.

Standing behind Ethan on the hover-scooter (and holding on to him for dear life), Connor called down to the girl as they zoomed over her head. 'Stay there! We'll get your bag back.'

If the girl replied, neither of the Space Detectives heard her above the hover-scooter's rumbling motors.

'I see it!' said Connor, and jabbed a spindly finger in the direction of a small purple blur in the distance. 'It's heading for the park.'

'Gotcha,' said Ethan, and revved the scooter's throttle hard. The motor growled and the vehicle received an extra burst of speed. 'What even is that purple thing, anyway?'

'A Tufted Grotsnobbler,' said Connor. 'I recognised it at once.'

'Of *course* you did.'

'They live on Venus and eat lava-berries. They're normally quite friendly.'

Ethan snorted. 'Well, this one isn't making any friends today.'

Before them lay the vast green expanse of

24

Starville's main park. The two boys could make out the leafy canopies of several tall trees, a silvery-blue lake bobbing with boats and several groups of people dotted here and there, sunbathing, playing games or enjoying picnics in the sun. Weaving between the trees and people – and showing no sign of tiring – was the Tufted Grotsnobbler.

'Looks like it's heading for the boating lake,' said Connor. 'Tufted Grotsnobblers can breathe underwater so maybe it's trying to hide in it. Cut across that path over there and let's try to head it off.'

Ethan wrenched the handlebars and the hover-scooter swerved frantically through the air. Entering the park, it whooshed narrowly over the heads of a pair of joggers, who shook their fists angrily after the speeding vehicle.

'We're gaining on it!' cried Ethan excitedly.

'Yes, but watch out for that tree!' said Connor.

'Tree?'

The underside of the hover-scooter clipped the top branches of a chestnut tree. The two boys felt a tremendous jolt and their vehicle was suddenly sent hurtling towards the ground.

'Pull up!' screamed Connor. 'Pull up now!'

'Yeah, that did occur to me, actually,' hissed Ethan, and pulled back hard on the handlebars. The hover-scooter's course levelled out, sending it skimming over the

grass, directly towards a family of picnickers lazing on a large tartan blanket.

'Probably a good idea to move, guys!' called Ethan.

With cries of alarm, the family scattered an instant before the growling hover-scooter tore through the picnic. Bits of food and paper plates flew messily in all directions. The tartan blanket snagged on the underside of the hover-scooter and began to drag along the grass.

SKKKKRANNNNNKKKKKKKKKKKKKK!

'Eurgh!' said Connor as he was pelted in the face by a dozen swamp-lizard drumsticks and half a plate of Venusian potato salad.

'Hey!' said Ethan, munching. 'Have you tried the snorgleberry drizzle cake? It's out of this world!'

'Forget the food and concentrate on where we're going!' yelled Connor.

The hover-scooter gained more height. Connor and Ethan spotted the Tufted Grotsnobbler slithering along a narrow footpath towards the boating lake.

Reaching down, Connor disentangled the tartan blanket from the underside of the hover-scooter. 'See if you can get directly over the creature. I'll drop the blanket on it. Tufted Grotsnobblers breathe out of little holes in the top of their heads, so that ought to slow it down a bit.'

'Nice idea, mate!'

Ethan pulled back hard again on the handlebars and the hover-scooter climbed into the sky. An alarm bleeped urgently.

'Oh dear,' said Ethan.

'Is that "Oh dear, we're nearly out of fuel" by any chance?' asked Connor.

'Afraid so,' said Ethan.

'Oh dear.'

'You'd better not miss with that blanket.'

'I'll try not to. Take us down as low as you can.'

The Tufted Grotsnobbler had nearly reached the boating lake. Ethan aimed the front of the hover-scooter downwards and, with a whine of motors, the vehicle descended sharply. Connor held the blanket ready. Now they were just a metre or two above the slimy purple beast …

'We're running on empty!' cried Ethan. 'It's now or never!'

Holding his breath, Connor dropped the blanket ...

... which landed straight on the Tufted Grotsnobbler, covering it completely. The creature skidded wildly, let out a blood-curdling bellow, collided with a tree trunk and finally rolled to a halt in a large, lumpy, tartan ball.

'We did—' began Connor triumphantly, but before he could add the word 'it', the hover-scooter plunged into the boating lake.

The two boys splashed and spluttered but quickly scrambled out of the water. Soaking and covered with pondweed, they dashed to where the Tufted Grotsnobbler lay motionless on the ground. Poking out from under the blanket was one striped corner of the girl's bag.

'Not the most challenging mystery to

solve,' said Ethan, reaching down to pick up the bag. 'But at least we can get this back to its rightful owner now.'

'I'm pretty sure we wouldn't have got this result without my extensive knowledge of the biology of Tufted Grotsnobblers,' said Connor.

'Yeah, all right, brainbox. We also wouldn't have caught it without my hover-scooter skills,' said Ethan. 'Speaking of which, we need to go fishing. That pile of scrap's going to need more than a full tank of fuel if it's ever going to fly again.'

But at that moment the Tufted Grotsnobbler suddenly sprang back to life with a savage snarl, throwing the tartan blanket aside. With its huge slimy claw, it snatched the girl's bag from Ethan. Then two tiny insect-like wings sprouted from the creature's back and began to beat rapidly.

With a low buzzing noise, the Tufted Grotsnobbler rose into the air. It hovered above the two boys, letting out a throaty, mocking laugh, then turned and streaked away over the treetops.

Ethan blinked and scraped a handful of pondweed from his hair.

'Oh, silly me,' said Connor. 'Forgot to mention. They can fly, too.'

Fifteen minutes later, pushing their waterlogged hover-scooter, the pair arrived back at the ice cream stall. There they found the girl with the pigtails and the animated cat T-shirt waiting for them.

'Really sorry,' said Ethan, 'we couldn't get your bag back. Despite one of us being a genius and the other being a hover-scooter whizz, we were outwitted by a Tufted Grotsnobbler.'

'Guys!' exclaimed the girl. 'You've both been so brave! I'm super-grateful for how you tried to help!'

'No problem,' said Ethan, shaking the girl's hand. 'I'm Ethan, by the way, and this is Connor.'

'Hi,' said the girl. 'I'm Edwina Snoddy.'

'We don't just sell ice cream,' said Connor, adjusting his glasses. 'We're the Space Detectives. I'm the clever one.'

Ethan groaned. 'And I'm the not-quite-as-clever-but-fun one. I hope you're not too upset after this incident, Edwina. Do you want us to call the Starville Police? Or your parents?'

'My mum is on her way now,' said Edwina. 'She'll know what to do about the bag. Hey – how'd you guys like to come to a party? As a little thank you for trying to help? We're having one tonight for Mum's birthday.'

Ethan's eyes lit up. 'Wow, that sounds brill! Thanks!'

Connor frowned. 'Oh, I already had plans to spend this evening memorising interesting facts about asteroids. To be honest, I'm not very keen on parties – they can get a bit noisy.'

Edwina grinned. 'Not even parties with virtual reality rollercoasters and a zero-gravity bouncy castle?'

Connor's eyes widened beneath his glasses. 'Oh. That sounds quite fun, actually.'

'Cool!' beamed Edwina. 'The address is Number One, Rocket Boulevard.'

There was a loud whine of antigravity engines and an enormous hover-car the size of a bus drew up to the ice cream stall. Protruding from its bonnet was a flag showing a white circle on a starry background – the emblem of Starville.

'Blimey!' exclaimed Ethan. 'That car belongs to the Supreme Governor of Starville, doesn't it?'

A hatch opened in the side of the hover-car and Edwina moved to climb in.

'What are you doing?' Ethan cried.

'It's OK. My mum is the Supreme Governor,' said Edwina.

Connor and Ethan exchanged a look of astonishment.

'Come on, Edwina!' boomed a deep female voice from within the huge vehicle. 'We haven't got all day!'

Edwina climbed through the hatch and turned to face the two boys. 'Catch you later, guys! Dress to impress!'

The hatch closed and the hover-car soared away.

Chapter 3

Friends in high places

The living room of Uncle Nick's house resembled a high-tech electronics shop after an earthquake. On every available surface, odd bits of wiring and strange parts of random machines lay scattered in piles.

Uncle Nick himself – a cheerful man in his early thirties with a bushy, tangled beard and whose face and clothes were never without oil stains – was busying himself by poking a screwdriver into Connor and Ethan's upturned hover-scooter.

There was a gurgling noise and a small torrent of smelly lake water gushed out of the handlebars.

'I've heard of a flooded engine,' said Uncle Nick, mopping up the spill with a grimy rag, 'but this is ridiculous.'

'We need to ask you something, actually, Uncle Nick,' said Ethan.

'Oh yes?'

'Yes. That girl, Edwina, who came to the stall today when we had the trouble with the ice cream machine? It turns out she's the daughter of the Supreme Governor of Starville! And she's invited me and Connor to a party tonight.'

'Goodness me!' cried Uncle Nick. 'The Supreme Governor! That old monster!'

'She's a monster?' said Ethan. 'Not a human, then?'

Uncle Nick gave a bitter chuckle. 'She's a human being, Ethan. Just not a very nice one. I used to be Starville's Chief Space Engineer, see? In charge of all the technology that keeps Starville functioning. When she came to power, she sacked all two hundred of us Space Engineers – every last human,

Martian Twig Person, Plutonian Cow Person and Tufted Grotsnobbler – and replaced us with robots to save money. Ha! Like that's a good idea! I told her no robot is a match for a real engineer, but she just laughed at me and said I was living in the past. Robots, indeed! I wouldn't be surprised if there's a serious malfunction with Starville's systems very soon.' He shook his head sadly. 'Anyway, enough of my moaning, lads. A party at the big house, eh? What do you need? Transport? I'll have the scooter up and running in no time.'

'We need to know what clothes to wear,' said Ethan. 'Edwina says we should dress to impress, but what does that mean exactly? Best jumpers? Suits? Bow ties?'

Uncle Nick leaped to his feet delightedly and started rummaging in a pile of junk. 'I have *just* the thing for you lads! Where are they? Ah, here we go!' He held up two saggy grey jumpsuits. 'These are what you want.'

'Erm, no disrespect,' began Ethan, eyeing the dull grey garments, 'but they don't look very smart.'

'I know,' said Uncle Nick, and tossed the saggy grey jumpsuits at the boys. 'They'll be just right. I promise. Stick 'em on over what you're wearing now.'

Exchanging puzzled glances, Connor and Ethan pulled on the stretchy jumpsuits.

'I can't imagine who these outfits would impress,' said Connor, looking at his reflection in a broken vending machine dumped in the corner of the room. 'We look like a pair of apprentice plumbers.'

Uncle Nick smirked. 'Here comes the good bit. Look at the left cuff of your outfits. What do you see?'

'A tiny keyboard,' said Ethan. 'With a little screen next to it. It's blank.'

'That's because the smartsuits aren't activated yet,' said Uncle Nick.

'Smartsuits?' echoed the two boys.

'That's right! Why fret over whether you're wearing the right outfit for any occasion when your clothes can automatically become whatever you need?'

Ethan couldn't stop himself from laughing. 'You're not serious?'

'Try me!' said Uncle Nick. 'This is a posh do, right? So type the words *formal party* into your cuff keyboards and see what happens.'

The boys did as Uncle Nick suggested. There was a pleasant electronic chiming noise and the surface of each smartsuit began to shimmer.

Then, with a final **PINNNNG** sound, the two dull grey jumpsuits suddenly transformed themselves into smart tuxedos complete with bow ties.

'Awesome!' cried Ethan, admiring his elegant new outfit. 'We look fantastic! What an incredible invention!'

'There's just one thing I don't understand, Nick,' said Connor, adjusting his glasses.

'Oh,' said Ethan. 'That's a first.'

'What's on your mind, laddie?' asked Uncle Nick.

'Why aren't you a billionaire?' asked Connor. 'If these smartsuits are as brilliant as they appear, surely every person in the known universe would want to buy one?'

Uncle Nick coughed and looked away. 'Ah. Yeah. Well. I tried to interest companies in my smartsuit technology but no one was having it. I think someone had been spreading rumours about my work not being up to scratch. Pound to a penny it was our friend the Supreme Governor again. One day all this tinkering with junk will pay off and I'll come up with an invention even better than the smartsuits. When that happens I'll buy you a brand-new top-of-the-range hover-scooter and you won't have to ride this old heap of junk.'

That evening, clad in their smartsuit tuxedos, Connor and Ethan arrived at the Supreme Governor's mansion on their newly repaired hover-scooter. The mansion was a tall, stony building – something between a castle and a pyramid – and was surrounded by a pleasant series of gardens filled with exotic plants. At the front entrance, humans and aliens in stylish outfits were streaming inside through an impressive set of double doors.

They were greeted by what looked like a very tall, muscly green anteater holding a clipboard. The creature stared down its long nose at them.

'Names?' it growled.

'Ethan Kennedy and Connor Crake,' said Ethan.

The anteater studied its clipboard. 'Your names aren't on my list!' it thundered. 'How dare you try to sneak into the Supreme Governor's mansion, you despicable little weasels! Scum like you have no place at a respectable event like this! I've a good mind to tear you limb from limb and throw your stinking remains into a – oh, my mistake,' it said, its voice suddenly turning friendly. 'There you are at the bottom of the list! Connor and Ethan. Sorry! Can't read my own writing! Please, go through! Have a lovely evening, chaps!' With a huge hairy paw, it beckoned them into the mansion.

Eager to get away from this strange animal, Connor and Ethan hurried inside.

They found themselves in a wide, crowded lobby decked out with tables and chairs. On one wall was a gigantic TV screen showing a slideshow of images featuring a tall woman in glasses. A caption underneath read:

Happy Birthday, Supreme Governor!

There was also a large number of cats in the lobby, fluffy, pampered-looking creatures with long white fur and haughty expressions. Around the edge of the lobby ran a tremendously long buffet table laden with every kind of food imaginable.

Mouth already watering, Ethan sped to the buffet and began to fill a shiny silver plate with food. One of the many cats hopped lightly on to the buffet table and purred at him. He ruffled the fur on the animal's head and examined a tag dangling from a collar around its neck.

My name is Tiger 5 and I belong to Edwina Snoddy.

'Hello, Tiger 5,' said Ethan. 'You'd better get down from this table or I expect you'll get into trouble.'

'Ethan!' hissed Connor, threading his way through the crowd towards him. 'If you can stop thinking about your stomach for five seconds, I've just made a very interesting discovery.'

'So have I,' said Ethan. 'I can stack thirty-nine chocolate digestives on this plate without them toppling over.'

'I've just seen a Tufted Grotsnobbler,' said Connor.

'Eek!' exclaimed Ethan with a jolt, which launched his thirty-nine chocolate digestives into the air. Tiger 5 gave a frightened yowl and bounded away. 'Is it the one from earlier?'

52

'Couldn't tell,' said Connor. 'It vanished into the crowd before I could check if it was wearing that ridiculous little cowboy hat. They're mostly friendly creatures, as I say, so it could be nothing. But if it is the one we encountered ...'

'It might not be happy about us chasing it,' said Ethan, his face turning pale. He dumped his now empty plate on the buffet table. 'I've suddenly lost my appetite.'

Connor nodded grimly. 'No point causing a fuss now and panicking everyone. But we should keep an eye out for any trouble.'

'Gotcha,' said Ethan. 'Ooh, my appetite's come back again.' He searched around for his scattered biscuits.

'There they are!' cried a familiar voice.

It was Edwina and she was with a stern-looking grown-up, whom they recognised as the tall, bespectacled woman from the slideshow playing on the big screen. Several white cats were milling around their feet.

'Mum, this is Ethan and Connor,' said Edwina. 'They're the two boys I was telling you about.'

'It's a great pleasure to meet you, Supreme Governor,' said Connor. 'And may we pass on our heartiest felicitations on this happy occasion.'

'Err, yeah,' agreed Ethan. 'What he said.'

Nose wrinkling, Edwina's mum, Supreme Governor Snoddy, peered at Connor and Ethan as if they were something one of Edwina's cats had coughed up. She gestured at Connor with a hand covered with gold rings. 'Why is that one dressed as a clown?' she asked coldly.

Connor blinked. 'Excuse me?'

'Blimey!' cried Ethan. 'Your smartsuit, Connor!' He scooped his silver plate off the table and held it up for his friend like a mirror.

Connor peered at his reflection in the plate and was shocked to find he was wearing a red-and-white-striped clown suit with a row of furry pom-poms down the front. 'What?' he spluttered. 'I look ridiculous!'

'Now I get it,' groaned Ethan. 'No wonder Uncle Nick couldn't get any companies to buy his smartsuits. They don't work properly! Try typing *formal party* into the cuff keyboard again.'

Desperately, Connor typed away at the keyboard on his sleeve. There was a weak **PLIPPPHT** sound and a black bow tie suddenly sprouted from the costume's collar.

'Great!' said Ethan. 'That's a start!'

But then the bow tie suddenly turned purple and began to spin.

'Ah,' said Ethan. 'Less great.'

Supreme Governor Snoddy glared at her daughter. 'Is this some kind of joke, Edwina? Parading a pathetic clown about at my birthday party? This is a very important occasion, you know. Are you trying to make a fool of me in front of the whole of Starville?'

'No!' cried Edwina, her face reddening. 'Of course not! You heard what they said. It's a wardrobe malfunction!'

'Pah!' spat Supreme Governor Snoddy. 'Once again you disappoint me, Edwina. Sometimes I wonder where I went wrong in your upbringing. I'll never be proud of you.'

Nose in the air, she strode away.

'Aaargh!' fumed Edwina, punching a trifle in frustration. 'My mum drives me potty! Nothing I do is ever, ever, ever, *ever* good enough!'

'Tough break,' said Ethan. 'Can't be easy having a Supreme Governor for a parent.'

'Oh, leave me alone, you pair of losers,' groaned Edwina, and stormed off into the crowd.

Determined to salvage some enjoyment from the evening, Connor and Ethan joined the queue for the zero-gravity bouncy castle. After a short time, they found themselves at the front.

'Great,' sighed Ethan. 'Now for some real fun!'

'Sorry! We've just been told to shut down all games and rides!' said the tall, orange-skinned Martian running the attraction, fastening a chain across its entrance and hanging up a little *Closed* sign. 'The Supreme Governor is about to cut her birthday cake and deliver a speech.'

Ethan shook his head at Connor and let out a groan. '*I don't believe it.* Edwina's upset with us. Your smartsuit goes haywire. And now we can't even go on this zero-g bouncy castle. Can this evening get any worse?'

A sudden burst of music blared and a grim-faced newsreader appeared on the lobby's big video screen. He did not look like he was about to sing 'Happy Birthday'.

'People of Starville,' said the newsreader.

BREAKING NEWS

'We face a terrible danger! It seems that for some unknown reason Starville has broken out of its orbit around the Earth and is now heading on a deadly collision course with the Moon!'

Connor adjusted his glasses. 'I'd say the answer to your question is yes, Ethan. The evening just got quite a bit worse.'

Chapter 4

Panic on the streets of Starville

There were screams and gasps from the partygoers. Many dashed madly to their vehicles parked outside, desperate to leave the space station.

'Furthermore,' continued the newsreader, 'all station airlocks and escape pods are mysteriously out of order. Unless a way can be found to alter Starville's course and prevent it smashing into the Moon, we are all doomed. The collision is expected to happen in a little under three hours' time. Stay tuned to this channel for updates.

In the meantime, here is some music ...'

There were more, even louder, screams and gasps. Now nobody rushed anywhere. There didn't seem any point. People just stood around, dazed by the awful news.

'You know that big brain of yours?' said Ethan, nudging Connor. 'Now might be a good time to crank it into gear and start thinking. What the flipping heck are we going to do?'

'It's a fascinating problem,' said Connor. 'I'm looking forward to figuring it out.'

'To you it's a fascinating problem. To the rest of us it's life and death! Any ideas?'

Connor frowned and adjusted his glasses. 'Space stations don't just fly out of orbit. Starville's rocket motors must have been fired to push it off into space. And it's too much of a coincidence that we're now heading straight for the Moon. That means we've been *aimed* at the Moon like an arrow at a target. And that means someone *did* this.'

'Sabotage?' said Ethan. 'But why?'

Connor shrugged. 'To hold Starville to

ransom? For revenge? For the sheer evil thrill of it? Any of your usual bad-guy reasons apply.'

'We'd better start investigating,' said Ethan. 'There isn't much time.'

'Some local knowledge would help,' said Connor. He glanced around and eventually spotted Edwina in the crowd. She was desperately hugging one of her many white fluffy cats. They waved to attract her attention.

'Hey, guys,' she said quietly, disentangling herself from the crowd and coming over to meet them. 'I'm so sorry I was rude to you earlier.'

'Hardly matters now, does it?' said Ethan brightly. 'We could all be dead in a few hours.'

'Speaking of which,' said Connor, 'we need your assistance.'

Edwina looked startled. 'My assistance?'

She placed the cat gently on the floor, where it gave a bored yawn and trotted away.

Connor nodded. 'We're certain some evil person has done this deliberately. But we might be able to stop this Moon-crashing business. Will you help us? You know Starville better than us, and your computer skills could be invaluable.'

Edwina bit her lip thoughtfully and then gave an emphatic nod. 'Count me in, guys. If there's anything I can do, just say. But you do realise – if some evil person or thing really is involved, sorting out this awful mess could be terribly, terribly dangerous?'

'That's fine,' said Ethan. 'Awful messes and terrible danger are two of our three favourite things.'

'What's the third one?' asked Edwina.

'Popcorn with Bolognese sauce.'

'Speak for yourself,' said Connor.

On Connor's instructions, she led them to a
luxurious living room where they gathered
around a computer placed on top of a
beautiful grand piano. Edwina swiped
a finger across the screen and downloaded
a detailed map of Starville. Around them,
more white cats padded haughtily. One
rubbed itself against Ethan's leg. He stooped
to read its name tag:

**My name is Sasha 12 and
I belong to Edwina Snoddy.**

'OK. So we're here,' said Connor, pointing to a large building near the very centre of the map. 'At the Supreme Governor's mansion. And we need to get *here*.' He tapped a finger on a large square building several streets away.

'Of course!' said Edwina. 'I see what you're doing! What a clever plan!'

'Either of you two geniuses care to explain this clever plan to a kid of average brainpower?' asked Ethan.

'It's my theory,' said Connor, 'that the current technical problems Starville is experiencing are down to a *computer virus* that someone has infected its computers with. You know, like how the Misty 54 virus caused our ice cream machine to go wrong.'

'Then why don't we tell someone in authority and get them to fix it?' asked Ethan.

Connor shook his head. 'But what if someone in authority is *behind* this? No. We need to handle this ourselves. Use Edwina's skills to neutralise the computer virus and then figure out who's to blame for this horrible situation.'

'But how … ?'

'We need to get inside the Central Computer Hub. That's this square building on the map *here*,' said Connor.

Edwina grinned delightedly at Ethan. 'I

bet I could erase that computer virus in twenty seconds flat if I was allowed access to Starville's central computer system!'

'Is it easy to get in there?' asked Ethan.

Edwina shook her head. 'Nope. Robot guards everywhere.'

'Then what we'll have to do,' said Ethan, 'is *sneak* in. Fortunately, I like sneaking.'

'Indeed!' said Connor. 'I also relish the thrill associated with covert activities.'

'I think that means he likes sneaking too,' said Ethan. 'How do we get into this Central Computer Hub place?'

Connor traced a line on the map with his finger. 'It seems there's a disused sewer tunnel that runs straight under the Central Computer Hub. There's even a hatch that opens from it into the building's basement.'

'Great,' said Ethan. 'If a bit pongy.'

'The map says it's been disused for years,'

said Connor. 'There shouldn't be a pong problem.'

'The only way into this disused sewer tunnel is through this hatch *here*,' said Connor, tapping a point on the map.

Ethan squinted at the screen. 'Does that say **Starville Space Zoo**?'

Connor nodded. 'Yes. And it seems to get into the tunnel we'll need to sneak into one of the zoo's animal enclosures.'

'Which enclosure exactly?'

Connor brought up a plan of Starville Space Zoo showing the animals in each enclosure. He pointed to one particular graphic. 'The hatch is located in the enclosure used to house *this* animal.'

Ethan's jaw sagged. The graphic showed a creature with a mixture of fur, horns, claws and scales. It looked a bit like a dragon wearing a fur coat.

A caption beside it read:

Snarltoothed Grizloid.
Carnivore. The most dangerous
animal in the known universe.

Edwina filled her striped bag with a few useful items and the three of them climbed aboard the Space Detectives' hover-scooter.

The streets were eerily deserted. Arriving at Starville Space Zoo, they found the gates unlocked and the ticket booth empty.

'Looks like everyone just dashed home to be with their families when they heard the bad news,' said Edwina as they parked the hover-scooter near the front entrance. 'Come on.' She hurried inside. The zoo was shrouded in shadows and silent, save for the occasional hoot of some exotic night bird.

'How long have we got until, you know, *Moon-splat-time*?' asked Ethan as he followed, glancing about nervously.

Connor looked at his watch. 'About two and three-quarter hours.'

'That's plenty,' said Edwina. 'The tough bit is going to be dealing with the Snarltoothed Grizloid.'

'Leave that to me,' said Connor brightly. 'I don't expect it'll be much of a problem.'

'Really?' said Edwina. 'You do know how big and dangerous these things are? They make Tufted Grotsnobblers look like baby mice in pink fluffy mittens.'

'I shall be using brain rather than brawn,' said Connor. 'I happen to have read Starville Central Library's only copy of **How to Look After Your Snarltoothed Grizloid** and I know exactly how to deal with them.'

'What are you going to do?' asked Ethan. 'Bore it to sleep with some of your interesting facts about asteroids?'

'*Ha ha*,' said Connor flatly. 'Actually, you're not so very far off. I shall be using *this*.' He removed a small metal object from the pocket of his clown suit. It was thin and silvery and had two long prongs rather like a blunt piece of cutlery.

'What's that?' asked Ethan.

Connor struck the metal object on the floor. The object's prongs quivered and made a pleasing chiming noise.

'It's a tuning fork,' explained Connor. 'People use them to keep their pianos in tune. It was on a table next to the Supreme Governor's grand piano. It's just what we need.'

'What are you gonna do?' asked Ethan. 'Sing it a lullaby?'

Connor nodded. 'Sort of. In a very scientific way. You see, the Snarltoothed Grizloid is usually found in the jade forests of Titan. As the sun goes down, the wind blows through the jade trees and it makes their leaves vibrate, producing the musical note we call middle C, the same note this tuning fork produces.'

Ethan gave a shrug. 'So what? You bang the fork on something and the creature feels homesick?'

'Not homesick,' said Connor. '*Sleepy*. The Snarltoothed Grizloid associates the sound of the jade forest leaves with sleep. Play the note middle C and our creature will instantly fall unconscious. That's the plan, anyway.'

'That's brilliant,' said Edwina. 'Totally brilliant!'

'Thank you,' said Connor. 'I do try not to have any ideas that *aren't* totally brilliant.'

The Snarltoothed Grizloid enclosure was a wide wooded space surrounded by a tall wire fence. There was no sign of the enclosure's fearsome inhabitant.

Ethan peered nervously through the wire mesh. 'How do we get through this fence? There's a keeper's gate over there leading inside. Can you hack the computer locking mechanism somehow, Edwina?'

She took out an enormous pair of scissor-like wire cutters from her rucksack. 'Actually, I have a simpler solution.'

Once inside the enclosure, the three children tiptoed delicately through the undergrowth. It was twilight and the bristling plants cast spooky shadows that danced over the grass. The air was very still.

'See those two tall trees in the distance?' whispered Connor. 'That square thing between them must be the hatch leading to the tunnel.'

'Maybe the creature's not even in here,' whispered Ethan hopefully. 'Perhaps it's poorly and had to spend the night at the space vet's.' He suddenly stumbled over a tree root and pitched face first on to the grass.

'Watch where you're going,' hissed Connor. 'We don't want to attract the creature's attention.'

'Yeah, I had sort of realised that,' whispered Ethan moodily in reply. 'Anyway, it wasn't my fault I fell over, it was this stupid tree root.' He gave the gnarled woody root a kick.

The root shuddered. And shivered. And swayed.

A harsh, stomach-churning howl filled the air.

Blood freezing, Ethan looked along the thick wriggling tree root and saw it was not so much a tree root as a *tail*, and that it was connected to an animal the size of a house. An animal with matted grey fur, horns like a rhinoceros, teeth like a shark and the slavering expression of a hungry crocodile.

'Now would be a good time to get out the tuning fork,' he croaked at Connor, barely able to speak.

'I agree one hundred per cent,' croaked Connor in reply. Hands trembling, he took out the tuning fork and flicked one of the metal prongs sharply with his finger.

The simple chiming note rang out.

The Snarltoothed Grizloid opened its mouth …

'It's working,' hissed Edwina excitedly. 'It's yawning!'

… then the beast exhaled a furious blast of fire at the tuning fork, melting it instantly. Rounding on the three children, the Snarltoothed Grizloid threw back its head and let out another terrible roar.

'Oh,' said Connor. 'I didn't know they could breathe fire.'

'I thought you read a book all about Snarltoothed Grizloids?' said Ethan, exasperated.

'Well, I read *most* of it,' said Connor. 'Now I think about it, I did skip a few chapters because I was so keen to start this brilliant new book I'd got about asteroids.'

Chapter 5
Hubbub
in the hub

Jaws slavering, the Snarltoothed Grizloid looked from Ethan to Connor to Edwina, as if trying to decide which child should be starter, which main course and which pudding.

'*Whistle!*' hissed Connor. 'Quickly!'

'I can't think of any tunes right now,' squeaked Ethan.

'He means whistle middle C, you idiot!' said Edwina. She pursed her lips and blew.

Connor did the same. Between them they produced a strong, steady note.

The Snarltoothed Grizloid regarded them curiously, and then its tiny eyes began to flicker. It shook its enormous head, as if trying to clear it.

Edwina and Connor's faces were turning red as they tried to keep their whistled note going as long as possible. They gestured desperately for Ethan to join in.

'Gotcha!' Ethan put his lips together and blew hard. They made only a tuneless rasping sound. He tried again, with the same result. 'I knew I shouldn't have eaten all those chocolate digestives!' he groaned. 'My mouth's all dry!'

While Connor was still whistling the note, his eyes scrunched shut and his face almost purple, Edwina took a deep gasping breath and then began whistling again, loud and strong. Now Connor took the chance to fill his lungs, and then he too began to whistle again in a clear, steady tone.

The Snarltoothed Grizloid closed its eyes and sank slowly on to the grass, its long scaly head between its two huge front paws like a sleeping dog. After a few seconds, its breathing became slow and regular. A tiny wisp of blue smoke trickled from one nostril.

Faces reddening again, Connor and Edwina continued whistling for as long as their lungs would allow. Slowly, the sound faded and the two children collapsed, panting, on to the grass.

'I think,' spluttered Edwina between gasps, 'it would probably have been easier to carry the grand piano here.'

The hatch opened easily and the three children quickly climbed down a metal ladder into a dingy tunnel. A row of dim lights attached to the ceiling stretched off into the far distance.

'This way,' said Edwina, and strode off into the gloom. 'And we should hurry. Every second matters.'

The two boys followed.

'Who would want to do something as horrible as sending Starville crashing into the Moon?' wondered Edwina as they made their way through the gloomy tunnel. 'Who would even have the expertise to do it?'

'Someone with great technical skills and a grudge against those in charge here, probably,' mused Connor.

Ethan tugged Connor's sleeve. 'You don't mean ... ?'

Connor shrugged. 'Your Uncle Nick's Starville Space Engineers? They have the know-how. And they're no friends of the Supreme Governor. Especially not Uncle Nick himself.'

'But he'd never put the lives of everyone on Starville at risk!' protested Ethan.

'Maybe not him. Maybe it's some rogue members of the organisation. Didn't he say a Tufted Grotsnobbler used to work there? Maybe that's the one that attacked Edwina.'

'Did you hear that?' said Ethan, suddenly skidding to a halt.

'Hear what?' asked Edwina.

'A squeak,' said Ethan.

Edwina shrugged. 'Probably just a garbage-rat. This is an old sewer, after all. Come on.'

They continued on their way.

After a short while, Ethan stopped again and raised a finger. 'There! I heard it again. A squeak. A really big one. Listen!'

SQUEEEEEEEEEEEE

Edwina sighed impatiently and listened. Connor listened too, silently polishing his glasses on one of the pom-poms of his clown suit.

EEEAKKKKKKK!

Edwina gave a gasp. 'I heard that! What the heck is it?'

Connor turned and pointed a spindly finger into the distance. 'There. Can you see? Heading this way.'

Rushing headlong down the tunnel towards them was a swarm of smallish grey creatures with leathery wings and tiny pointed teeth. Their bodies were fat and furry and they had long grey tails that twitched and thrashed.

'Amazing!' breathed Connor. 'A flock of Neptunian Bat-Rats! I suspect they escaped from the zoo some time ago and started a new colony down here.'

'They look hungry to me,' said Ethan. 'What do they eat?'

'In a word,' said Connor, '*us*. We should probably run for our lives now.'

Feet pounding on the metal floor, hearts thumping in their chests, the three children raced along the gloomy tunnel. Behind them, squeaking and chittering madly, swarmed the flock of Neptunian Bat-Rats, their tiny mouths snapping savagely.

'They're getting closer!' groaned Ethan, chancing a quick backwards glance.

SQUEAK!

SQUEAK!

SQUEAK!

SQUEAK!

'There's the hatch!' cried Edwina. 'But there's no ladder! How will we get up there?'

'I think I can probably reach it,' said Connor, and stretched up with his long spindly arms. His fingertips brushed the metal of the hatch …

'Hurry!' shouted Edwina.

Connor jumped, slamming the underside of the hatch with the palms of his hands. The hatch popped open on its hinge, flooding the tunnel with light.

The flapping and squeaking of the Bat-Rats grew louder with every second …

'Climb up!' yelled Connor.

'But there's no ladder!' said Edwina.

'Climb up *me*, I mean!' said Connor. 'You can hang on to the pom-poms on my clown suit!'

Nimbly, Edwina scrambled up Connor's body and through the hatch. Ethan followed, but Connor's long legs began to buckle under his friend's weight. Edwina tugged Ethan's collar and he scrambled up to safety. Then they each took one of Connor's hands and hauled him through the hatch and up into the light.

The screeching of the Bat-Rats was now thunderously loud.

'The hatch!' cried Connor.

Ethan lunged at the hatch and slammed it shut. There was a loud **CLANNNG** and the noise of the Bat-Rats was silenced.

'That was actually very interesting,' said Connor. 'I've always wanted to see a flock of Neptunian Bat-Rats.'

'Me too,' said Ethan. 'Just not when they thought I was their dinner.' He looked over at Edwina. 'What now?'

They were in a large storeroom filled with odds and ends of computer equipment.

Built into one wall was a keyboard and screen. Opposite was a lift giving access to the upper floors. She hurried to the computer and tapped a few keys. 'I can access the main computer system from here. It should let me find out exactly what the problem is ...' The computer gave a bleep. 'Wow!' cried Edwina. 'This is fantastic, guys!'

'What is?' asked Connor and Ethan together.

'The thing causing Starville's guidance system to go wrong. The thing that's going to make this place smash into the Moon – it's the Misty 54 virus!'

'The one that made our ice cream machine go bonkers?' asked Ethan. 'Perhaps this is something to do with Uncle Nick after all ... ?'

'That's the one!' said Edwina. 'It's a rather more complicated version of it. And it's really sneakily hidden in the computer code, which is probably why nobody's spotted it yet. But I'm sure I can fix it from here!' Her face suddenly fell. '*Uh-oh.*'

'Uh-oh what?' asked Ethan.

'According to this screen there's a bunch of robot guards on their way down in the lift to nab us.'

'You fix the computer,' said Ethan. 'We'll fix the guards.' He tugged Connor's sleeve and led him towards the lift.

'How are we going to do that?' asked Connor.

'Good question,' said Ethan, staring at the rapidly descending floor numbers on the screen above the lift's doors. 'Can you use that big brain of yours to bamboozle them with logic?'

Connor shrugged. 'Maybe. If they're in the mood to listen.'

The lift pinged and its doors slid open.

But there weren't any robots in the lift. There was just a single creature. A single, large, slimy, purple creature with nasty sharp teeth. It was wearing a small cowboy hat covered in shiny sequins.

The Tufted Grotsnobbler slithered out of the lift and advanced on them.

'There's a perfectly logical explanation for why we're here!' stammered Connor.

The creature shot out two large purple claws and grasped a boy in each.

'I don't think it cares about explanations,' said Ethan.

The purple creature slithered to the wall and opened a large metal chute. A label above it read **SPACE DISPOSAL TUBE**. It dumped the two boys inside.

'Does "Space Disposal Tube" mean what I think it does?' asked Ethan.

There was a loud hiss and a trapdoor opened in the bottom of the metal chute. There was a deafening rush of air as Connor and Ethan were fired out into the empty blackness of space.

Ah yes, thought Ethan as he passed out. *It does mean that.*

Chapter 6
Rather a whopper

Connor and Ethan wheeled silently through space, limp as rag dolls. Around them blazed a trillion tiny pinpricks of starlight.

Swiftly and calmly, Connor reached over and took hold of Ethan's arm. With freezing fingers, he quickly typed the word *space* into the keyboard on Ethan's wrist. Immediately, Ethan's tuxedo shimmered and transformed itself into a spacesuit, complete with oxygen tank. He typed the same word into his own cuff keyboard, hoping it would work. After an agonising pause, during which Connor felt the last wisps of air draining from his lungs, his clown suit finally dissolved away and was replaced by a silvery spacesuit.

Ethan's eyes flicked open. He found himself drifting gently through a black void. On one side of him was the emptiness of space, dotted with stars, a huge silvery orb gleaming. The Moon. It all looked very pretty. On the other side of him was an endless metal wall covered with bolts and rivets. The underside of Starville. His memory returned in a rush. Of course! They were outside the space station! It was all the fault of that awful Tufted Grotsnobbler ...

There was a crackling noise and a voice chirped from a small speaker inside his space helmet.

'Ethan? Can you hear me?'

It was Connor. Ethan twisted around and found his friend floating beside him. Connor gave a wave.

'Hi. Luckily, your Uncle Nick's smartsuits have a spacesuit mode.'

'But yours is faulty!' said Ethan. 'We need to get back inside before it turns into a clown costume again!'

Connor pointed a thick-gloved hand along the metal underside of Starville. 'I can see an emergency airlock over there. We just need to grab hold of something, aim ourselves at it and push off. We should float straight at it.'

Ethan squinted into the distance. 'That airlock's miles away! It'll take us ages to get there!'

'You have something more important to do?'

The two boys took hold of a large radio dish protruding from the metal surface. They braced themselves against it, knees bent, and then straightened their legs. Like stones from a slingshot, they flew towards the airlock. 'I hope Edwina's OK,' said Ethan. 'That Tufted Grotsnobbler doesn't know when to quit.'

'We should alert the Starville Police as soon as we get back on-board,' said Connor.

'Oh, by the way,' said Ethan. 'Wheeeeee! Floating through space is fun!'

'This is a life-or-death situation,' said Connor. He tried to adjust his glasses but his hand bounced off the face shield of his space helmet. 'This is not the time for fun.'

'Wheeeeeeeeeeeee!'

'It is fun, though, isn't it? You're having the time of your life right now, aren't you, mate? Admit it.'

Beneath the thick glass of his space helmet, Connor smiled shyly. 'Perhaps.'

A passage leading from the airlock opened on to the large tree-lined square in Starville's main shopping district, not far from their ice cream stall. The square was deserted and they searched in vain for a police officer. Suddenly a blast of happy music rang out.

'Wonderful news!' cried a voice. The two boys retracted their space helmets and looked up to see a large video billboard showing a news programme. 'Starville is saved! And all thanks to the marvellous computer programming skills of a very bright young girl called Edwina Snoddy!'

The video billboard showed a beaming Edwina standing beside her mother, Supreme Governor Snoddy. It took Connor and Ethan a moment to recognise Supreme Governor Snoddy because she was actually smiling.

'Tell us,' said a reporter, shoving a microphone under Edwina's nose, 'how did you do it?'

'I suspected sabotage from the beginning,' replied Edwina. 'Probably some kind of computer virus. I study computer viruses in my spare time, you see, so—'

'The girl's a genius,' said Supreme Governor Snoddy, swiping the microphone from her daughter. 'Top of the class in all her school lessons! I couldn't be prouder of her!'

GENIUS GIRL SAVES STARVILLE!

'Anyway,' said Edwina, taking back the microphone, 'I managed to locate and destroy the virus program that had taken over Starville's navigation system and program in a new course that will take us away from the Moon and back into orbit around the Earth.'

The animated image of the cat on Edwina's T-shirt disappeared and was replaced by a long scrolling string of numbers and letters.

'And I believe this text we can now see on your T-shirt is the actual new course you have plotted in for Starville to take!' said the reporter.

'Yes, it is,' said Edwina with a shy smile. 'A rather clever piece of programming, even if I do say so myself.'

'So proud!' said Supreme Governor Snoddy, leaning down to get close to the microphone. 'So proud of my clever, clever daughter!'

Connor blinked at the screen and adjusted his glasses.

'Who do you think is responsible for trying to send us hurtling into the Moon?' asked the reporter.

'It's not for me to point the finger at anyone,' said Edwina, 'but when I was erasing the virus file, I think – only *think*, mind, I can't be positive – I think I saw the words *Long Live the Starville Space Engineers* flash up on the screen. Perhaps that's a clue of some sort?'

'Aha!' cried the reporter. 'It's known that the Starville Space Engineers are no friends of the Supreme Governor.'

'Horrible bunch of good-for-nothings!' yelled Supreme Governor Snoddy into the microphone. 'I should have guessed they'd be behind this outrage!'

'Have you informed the Starville Police of this, Edwina?' asked the reporter.

'I have,' said Edwina. 'And I believe the Starville Police are rounding up members of the Starville Space Engineers for questioning.'

'Good to hear!' said the reporter. 'So with the joyful news that Starville is saved from destruction and steps are being taken to bring those responsible to justice, we hand you back to the studio ...'

'Did you hear that?' said Ethan. 'They think the Starville Space Engineers are responsible! They probably think Uncle Nick's behind the plot to destroy Starville!'

'That doesn't matter right now,' said Connor.

'Doesn't matter?' spluttered Ethan. 'What kind of a Space Detective are you? Starville may be saved but we still haven't found the culprit.'

'But we're not saved.'

'What? What are you on about?'

Connor adjusted his glasses. 'Those calculations on the screen showing how Edwina is sending Starville away from the Moon and back into Earth orbit? I checked them in my head and they're wrong.'

Ethan frowned. 'How wrong, exactly?'

'Quite catastrophically wrong. If Starville is sent on the course Edwina claims to have programmed, it will veer away from the Moon, head back to Earth, orbit around it once and then swing back straight towards the Moon. Where it will crash.'

'So, she hasn't saved us at all?'

'No,' said Connor. 'At the most she's bought us a few hours' time. Starville is still in terrible danger.'

There was a large crowd bustling outside the Supreme Governor's mansion, eager for more news about how Edwina Snoddy had saved Starville and the lives of every single being aboard it. The muscly green anteater was doing its best to shoo people away.

'Push off!' it yelled at a group of teenagers who were trying to peek in through one of the mansion's windows. 'Or I'll personally kick your butts into hyperspace.'

While the creature was occupied, Connor and Ethan sidled up to the mansion's big double doors.

'Hey! You two!' called the anteater. 'Where do you think you're going?'

Before they could think up an excuse, the creature bounded up to them on its thick legs. 'Oh, it's *you!*' it cried in a friendly voice. 'Connor and Ethan! I won't make the same mistake twice! Go straight in, me old mates!' It held open one of the heavy double doors.

The two Space Detectives slipped through the door before it could change its mind.

Once inside, they threaded their way through the crowd of partygoers, scouting for Edwina. Eventually, they found her lounging on a beanbag, eating an enormous bowl of ice cream. She was surrounded by fluffy white cats.

'Hello,' said Connor and Ethan in unison.

Edwina looked up and gave a start, nearly falling off her beanbag. Several of the cats screeched and scampered away.

'Guys! You made it! I was so shocked

when that Tufted Grotsnobbler came out of the lift ...'

'Never mind that,' said Connor, adjusting his glasses. 'You got your sums wrong, Edwina. This space station is still going to crash into the Moon.'

'Impossible!' cried Edwina, toying nervously with her pigtails. 'I don't make mistakes.'

'You made one this time,' said Connor. 'Rather a whopper too.'

Edwina leaped to her feet. 'Right. Come with me. I'll show you how I did it. I *think* I know why you believe I made a mistake, Connor, but if I can show you my working-out on my laptop, I'm positive I can change your mind. This way.'

She led them up a winding staircase towards her bedroom. More fluffy white cats were lazing on the landing. One trotted alongside Ethan. He bent down and patted it, swivelling the creature's collar towards him so he could read its name tag. A terrible thought suddenly occurred.

He tapped Connor on the arm and showed him the cat's name tag. Connor's eyes widened with interest. 'But ... !'

Before he could finish his sentence, Edwina swung open her bedroom door. 'In here, guys. This won't take a minute.'

Connor and Ethan stepped inside. It was large and comfortable with posters on the white-painted walls and many big fluffy cushions dotted about. There was also a large, angry Tufted Grotsnobbler wearing a sparkly cowboy hat in the room. It raised its claws at them and bellowed loudly.

Edwina stepped back out of the room and locked the door with a loud click.

'Why is it,' asked Ethan, as the slimy purple creature advanced on them, 'every time we think we're getting somewhere with this mystery, a flipping Tufted Grotsnobbler pops up and tries to kill us?'

'Just what I was wondering,' sighed Connor.

Chapter 7
Pick one

The two boys raced around the bed, putting it between themselves and the creature. With a single claw, the Tufted Grotsnobbler sliced the bed in two as easily as a sandwich, scattering pillows everywhere.

Slowly, it began to back Connor and Ethan into a corner, claws poised, hideous mouth leering, savouring its moment of triumph.

This time there was no escape.

Connor felt himself begin to tremble all over. 'Oh, just FYI,' he said through quivering lips, 'I've solved the mystery. I know who is behind this.'

'Me too,' said Ethan. 'The name of that cat outside the door turned out to be the vital clue we needed, didn't it?'

'Just a pity we're going to die horribly before we'll get the chance to tell anybody.'

The Tufted Grotsnobbler let out a terrifying roar.

'That's odd,' said Connor. 'My left foot seems to be trembling a lot more than the rest of me. I wonder why.'

'As mysteries go,' said Ethan, 'it doesn't sound all that urgent, mate.'

Connor unfastened the left boot of his spacesuit and peered inside. 'Looks like we have a stowaway. It must have fallen asleep in there.' A small fat grey thing with wings fluttered drowsily out of the boot and perched on top of a wardrobe.

'Oh no!' cried the Tufted Grotsnobbler in a high, piping voice. 'That's one of those

Neptunian Bat-Rats! I hate them! Please don't let it get me!' The huge purple creature slithered quickly into the corner of the bedroom and cowered.

'What?' laughed Connor. 'A big tough thing like you scared of one measly Neptunian Bat-Rat? They might be frightening in a flock – but *one*?'

'I can't help it!' yelped the Tufted Grotsnobbler. 'They've got horrible tails and nasty little eyes! They freak me right out and I just hate, hate, *hate* them!'

'Excellent!' said Ethan. He turned to his friend. 'Connor – would you? You're taller than me.'

'My pleasure,' said Connor. He jumped up and scooped the Neptunian Bat-Rat from the top of the wardrobe, careful to face its tiny snapping mouth away from him. Holding it at arm's length, he slowly advanced on the quaking Tufted Grotsnobbler in the corner of the room. 'There are two ways we can do this,' he said pleasantly. 'You can either tell us what we need to know right now. Which will be very quick and easy ...'

'Or,' said Ethan, 'we can lock you in a cupboard with this Neptunian Bat-Rat. Pick one.'

The evening air was pleasant and still as Supreme Governor Snoddy stepped into the mansion's roof garden. She gazed down at the now peaceful streets of Starville.

'So,' said a voice. 'I got your message. Why did you want to meet me here? It's all very mysterious.'

The Supreme Governor looked up to find Edwina sitting on a stone bench, surrounded by several of her cats. 'What do you mean?' she demanded. 'I didn't send you any message. *You* asked to meet *me* here, Edwina.'

Edwina shook her head, puzzled. 'No, I didn't.'

'Really?' Supreme Governor Snoddy frowned. 'How very odd.'

'Hello!' cried a high, piping voice. The purple Tufted Grotsnobbler slithered out of the shadows.

Edwina and her mother glared at the beast. 'You did this?' they chorused.

'Not me,' said the Tufted Grotsnobbler. 'I'm just obeying orders.'

'Good evening,' said a tall man wearing the dark blue uniform of the Starville Police as he popped out from behind a palm tree. 'I'm Chief Inspector Hill. Mind if I join you?'

Supreme Governor Snoddy swung to face him. 'Did you arrange this meeting, Chief Inspector?'

Chief Inspector Hill gave a little chuckle. 'Afraid not. I was invited here to make sure justice is done. The people who invited you are—'

'Are *us*,' said Connor as he and Ethan emerged from a darkened doorway on their hover-scooter. 'Hello. We're the Space Detectives.'

'Oh, thank goodness you two are OK!' said Edwina, rushing over to hug them.

'Not so fast,' said Ethan, dodging her embrace. 'We've got a mystery to unravel here. Connor?'

Connor stepped forward and pushed his glasses further up his nose. 'Pay attention, everyone. As you know, earlier today Starville left its normal orbit around the Earth and was sent on a deadly collision course with the Moon. This was no accident. Someone aimed this space station at the Moon, intending to cause a horrible disaster. Someone who is in this garden right now. Someone who had everything to gain from the crisis that followed.'

Edwina poked a finger at the Tufted Grotsnobbler. 'No doubt, this purple lump is behind it all. Probably in league with the Starville Space Engineers. They've had a grudge against Mum since she booted them all out of their jobs. They'd have the know-how to send us crashing into the Moon.'

'Now wait a minute,' began the Tufted Grotsnobbler in its high voice. 'This is very unfair ...'

'Come along now,' said Chief Inspector Hill, whipping out his electro-handcuffs.

'No need for the handcuffs just yet, Inspector,' said Connor. 'This creature is not the villain here. A human being is behind all this.'

Edwina gasped and turned to the Supreme Governor. 'Mum! It was you, wasn't it? Of course!'

Supreme Governor Snoddy gave a loud snort. 'What? *Me?* Are you serious?'

'It all makes sense now, Mum,' said Edwina, shaking her head sadly. 'You sabotaged Starville's guidance system and then thought you could blame it on the Starville Space Engineers. You've never liked them, have you? That way you'd have the perfect excuse to lock them all up once and for all. Oh, Mum. How could you?'

'This is absolute nonsense!' said the Supreme Governor, her face turning a deep red. 'A complete lie from start to finish! How dare you accuse your own mother of such vile wrongdoing!'

Chief Inspector Hill raised his eyebrows at Connor. 'Shall I arrest the lady now, then?'

Connor shook his head. 'It wasn't the Supreme Governor.'

'It wasn't?' asked Edwina.

'No.'

'Then who was it?' she demanded. 'Not this police chappie, surely?'

Connor fixed her with a stare. 'It was you, Edwina. You did this. You sent Starville on a deadly collision course with the Moon.'

'Me?' Edwina blinked and spluttered like a person who's just tripped unexpectedly into a swimming pool. '*Me? Are you completely boneheaded?*'

Ethan folded his arms. 'It *was* you, Edwina.'

Edwina opened her mouth but then closed it again. She glared at the two boys. 'Yes, all right,' she mumbled. 'I did it. Big deal.'

'Edwina!' exploded Supreme Governor Snoddy. 'How could you?'

'I knew you'd overreact,' groaned Edwina.

'Overreact?' bellowed her mother. 'You could have killed a million people! What do you expect me to say? *Oh there, there. Never mind?*'

Edwina heaved a long, weary sigh. 'Nothing I've ever done in my life has been good enough for you! It didn't matter if I got top marks in school or a hundred certificates for good behaviour. I won a gold medal in ski-bingo and you never even said congratulations. You always found some reason to criticise me. What does it take to impress this person? I wondered. So I hatched a plan. I would secretly send Starville flying off towards the Moon – and I would be the one to save it. I even tricked these two detective bozos into helping me. Made them think *I* was helping *them*. And it worked! It really worked. You were proud of me, weren't you, Mum?'

'I was,' said Supreme Governor Snoddy. She sniffed loudly. 'That didn't last long, did it?'

'But how did she do it?' asked Chief Inspector Hill. 'And how did you two work it out?'

Connor went over to the bench where

Edwina was sitting and picked up one of the fluffy white cats. Stroking its head, he checked its name tag. 'This cat helped us solve the mystery, actually.'

'It must be cleverer than it looks,' said Chief Inspector Hill.

'Tell everyone this cat's name, Edwina,' said Connor, and handed her the fluffy white creature.

Edwina took the cat and ruffled its fur. 'We keep pedigree cats and they each have a name and number to formally identify them. This one is **Misty 54**.'

'The same name as the computer virus,' said Ethan. 'What an amazing coincidence, eh?'

'Except, of course, it's no coincidence,' said Connor. 'The computer virus is called Misty 54 because Edwina *named it after her cat!* You see, Edwina created the virus herself – she's a computer genius, after all – and she used that computerised smart T-shirt she wears to beam it into our ice cream machine and into Starville's navigation systems, taking them both over.'

'Why did she need to take over our ice cream machine?' asked Ethan. 'I don't get why that needed to be part of her plan?'

'It didn't,' said Edwina. 'It was just fun seeing you two dweebs get squirted with ice cream.'

'So why did we need to sneak into the Central Computer Hub when you could have erased the virus from anywhere on Starville using that smart T-shirt of yours?'

'I needed to be the brave hero who risked everything to save the day,' said Edwina, 'and that scatty plan of getting into the hub via the zoo was just the thing.'

Ethan glared at her. 'We nearly got eaten by a Snarltoothed Grizloid!'

She shrugged. 'Yeah, well, you didn't, so stop whining.'

'Just one thing I don't understand,' said Chief Inspector Hill, and gestured at the Tufted Grotsnobbler, which had been watching them in silence. 'Where does this creature figure in all this?'

The purple creature cleared its throat. 'I do have a *name*, you know. It's Alice.'

'Sorry, Alice,' said Chief Inspector Hill. 'So, what's your story?'

'She's my adopted sister, if you must

know,' piped up Edwina. 'And she's always been the favourite. She's such a goody-goody.'

'But we saw her attacking you by the ice cream stall,' said Ethan. 'She stole your bag!'

'Ah,' said Edwina. 'Actually, that's Alice's bag. I've always liked it, so I sort of *borrowed* it this morning.'

'I got a bit annoyed when I found out,' said Alice, 'so I followed Edwina into town and snatched it back from her. That's when you two guys got involved.'

'But why didn't you tell us she's your sister and it was your bag the whole time?' asked Ethan.

Alice gave the Tufted Grotsnobbler version of a shrug. 'I get a bit nervous and tongue-tied sometimes and often I find myself just roaring savagely at people. It's something I need to work on, I realise that.'

'And the trying to kill us stuff? In the computer hub? And just now?'

'I'd have rescued you from space before you came to any real harm. Edwina just wanted to give you guys a bit of a scare. I like helping my sister, even if she is a teeny bit evil sometimes.'

'Right,' cried Edwina, leaping to her feet. 'You've had your fun working out my brilliant plan. Sorry I got my sums wrong and you're still going to crash into the Moon. I really should learn to check my work! I'll be off to my private escape pod now! Ta-ta, losers!'

She pushed the boys off their hover-scooter, leaped on to it and twisted the throttle hard.

Nothing happened.

Edwina frowned and kicked the hover-scooter.

'We took the battery out,' said Connor, adjusting his glasses. 'We've also informed the authorities that Starville's course still needs correcting. The engineers are on their way. So I think that's all your evil plans foiled.'

'Ha!' cried Ethan. 'That's what happens when you mess with the Space Detectives!'

Edwina shut her eyes slowly. 'Beaten by a pair of absolute boneheads. How embarrassing.'

Chief Inspector Hill reached again for his electro-handcuffs. 'Just want to make sure. I'm definitely arresting the one with the pigtails, yeah?'

'Definitely,' said Connor and Ethan together.

EPILOGUE

It was a smart new office halfway up a glitzy skyscraper in a swish part of town.

It had cost a lot of money to deck out with the very latest computer, fingerprint analysers, DNA sequencers, candyfloss dispensers (Ethan's idea) and other high-tech crime-fighting equipment, but Supreme Governor Snoddy had been very grateful to the two boys who had saved Starville from destruction and felt, if they had the right gear, there were more important things they could be doing with their time than selling ice cream.

An alert bleeped and Connor and Ethan dashed to their computer. As they read the email that had just arrived, their mouths began slowly to open in wonder.

The **Space Detectives** had a new case ...

COULD YOU BE A
SPACE
DETECTIVE?

HAVE YOU BEEN PAYING ATTENTION?

TAKE THE QUIZ AND FIND OUT!

1. What flavour ice cream do the Plutonian Cow People like best?

    a) Extra Minty Grapefruit and Smoky Bacon

    b) Salted Caramel Cheese and Tomato

    c) Triple Chocolate Broccoli Swirl

2. What was the name of the virus that caused the ice cream to malfunction?

    a) Misty 34

    b) Misty 44

    c) Misty 54

3. What colour is a Tufted Grotsnobbler?

    a) Purple

    b) Blue

    c) Pink

4. What fact about Tufted Grotsnobblers did Connor forget?

    a) They are from Venus

    b) They can breathe underwater

    c) They can fly

5. What job did Uncle Nick use to have?
  a) Chief Space Robot Operator
  b) Chief Space Engineer
  c) Chief Space Door Opener

6. What animals were there a lot of at the Supreme Governor's party?
  a) Rats
  b) Cats
  c) Bats

7. What is Ethan's third favourite thing?
  a) Popcorn with Bolognese sauce
  b) Awful messes
  c) Danger

8. Who couldn't whistle because they'd eaten too many chocolate digestives?
  a) Ethan
  b) Edwina
  c) Connor

9. What are Tufted Grotsnobblers scared of?
  a) Snarltoothed Grizloids
  b) Humans
  c) Neptunian Bat-Rats

10. Who changed the orbit of Starville so it would collide with the Moon?
  a) Uncle Nick
  b) Edwina
  c) Supreme Governor Snoddy

**LOOK OUT FOR ANOTHER
INTERGALACTIC MYSTERY**

IN

SPACE DETECTIVES

EXTRA WEIRD CREATURES

COMING SOON!

Read on for a sneak peek ...

PROLOGUE

PING!

Somewhere in Starville, a text message arrived on someone's mobile communicator. It was late – past midnight – and the owner of the mobile communicator had been in bed, asleep. Blearily, they reached for the device and read the message.

IS IT DONE???

Yawning, and with tired, fumbling fingers, the owner of the device typed a reply.

YES. WE SHOULD SEE
RESULTS IN THE MORNING.

A pause. Then another message pinged in.

EXCELLENT!!! OUR FIENDISH
PLAN NEARS COMPLETION! TOGETHER
WE SHALL BRING
CHAOS, CONFUSION AND MISERY TO THE
INHABITANTS OF STARVILLE – AND GROW
STAGGERINGLY
RICH IN THE PROCESS!
HAHAHAHAHAHAHAHAHAHAHA!

After a few seconds, it added:

NIGHTY-NIGHT, THEN.

The owner of the communicator put down the device and slumped back on to their pillow. Soon, they were deeply and comfortably asleep.

Chapter 1

Felix Plum is unwell

Mrs Plum rapped her knuckles three times on Felix's bedroom door.

'Your breakfast will be in the kitchen in five minutes, darling, or in the cat in ten. Up to you.'

Through the door there came a low, muffled groan.

Mrs Plum heaved a sigh. She'd seen hundred-year-old giant tortoises with more get-up-and-go than her son. She knocked again.

'Come on. The rocket bus will be here at eight thirty.'

'I don't wanna go to school,' came Felix's voice.

'It's the last week of term. You want to see all your friends, don't you?'

'I don't want to do anything. I feel funny and I've got a headache.'

'Oh, not that old fib,' sighed Mrs Plum. 'You realise kids have been trotting out that excuse since the dawn of history? I bet kids in caves used it to pull sickies from hunting mammoths. Come on, Felix. Stop wasting time.'

'I really have, Mum. I don't feel well. *At all.*'

Mrs Plum frowned. Normally Felix would snap out of his laziness, but today something felt different. A sudden thought occurred. Her son couldn't actually be ill? Could he?

She pushed open the door. Felix lay sprawled on the bed under an untidy heap of cushions and pillows, the duvet pulled over his head. Gently, she sat on the edge of the bed and cleared her throat.

'Felix, darling? Come out from under there, please.'

A small pair of hands appeared over the top edge of the duvet and pulled it down a few inches, revealing a scruffy mop of brown hair and a pair of watery blue eyes.

'Good heavens!' cried Mrs Plum. 'You look terrible, darling!' She laid a hand on Felix's forehead. 'And you have a temperature, too! You really are poorly! Is your head terribly painful?'

The boy nodded. 'Yeah. And there's this really weird feeling in my shoulder. I don't know what it is.'

'Oh dear. Let me see.'

Felix sat up and pulled down the duvet.

Mrs Plum gave a startled gasp and backed

away from the bed. 'Oh my goodness!'

Felix yawned. 'Hmm? What's up?' He noticed his mum was staring, horrified, at his right shoulder. He swivelled his head to see what she was looking at – and let out a blood-curdling scream.

Chapter 2
Head boy

High above the planet Earth floated the gigantic space station known as Starville. It was a single vast city enclosed under a great glass dome, a breathtakingly beautiful place of long elegant streets and lush green parks, home to over a million humans and aliens. The most astounding place in the whole solar system.

Located halfway up a glittering skyscraper in one of Starville's fancier districts was the office of the Space Detectives. Connor Crake and Ethan Kennedy were two ten-year-old boys from Earth who were staying on

Starville with Ethan's uncle Nick for the summer holidays. The pair had always been keen mystery solvers and, after recently saving Starville from an evil plot to send it crashing into the Moon, they had been given this marvellous office filled with the very latest detecting technology by Starville's grateful Supreme Governor.

Ethan was sitting behind his desk on his swivel chair, spinning rapidly, giggling as the world flashed by in a blur. His shirt front was streaked with filling from the pastry he'd eaten for breakfast. He was a short, squat boy with the nervous energy of a puppy.

'Will you stop doing that?' asked Connor irritably, adjusting his thick-lensed glasses. He was taller and thinner than Ethan and was sitting nearby at his own desk, studying the local news on his computer screen. 'It's incredibly distracting. One of these days you'll spin so fast you'll take off like a rocket-copter and fly out of the window.'

Ethan grabbed hold of the edge of his desk and the rapidly rotating chair came to an abrupt halt. He shook his head, which was woozy after all the spinning, and gave an apologetic shrug. 'Sorry, mate. I'm just so flipping bored. We've had nothing decent to investigate all week.'

This was true, Connor knew. In the past few days, the Space Detectives had solved a grand total of three mysteries, none of which had offered much of a challenge to their powers of investigation. He brought up the case notes on his computer screen to remind himself:

MYSTERY	SOLUTION
Stolen antique ring	Found inside slipper under bed

MYSTERY	SOLUTION
Ghost of Winston Churchill spotted in hallway	Reflection in hallway window from TV in building opposite showing Earth History Channel

MYSTERY	SOLUTION
Horrid smell in kitchen	Horrid, out-of-date cheese in fridge

Nothing to tax the minds of two bright young detectives there. In addition to being ridiculously easy to crack, these three cases shared something else in common. They had all been brought to Connor and Ethan's attention by the same person – a rather scatty old woman called Florence Quail, who lived by herself in the apartment next to their office. She was a kindly soul, often stopping by to bring the boys home-baked cookies, but Connor and Ethan had begun to wonder whether she was inventing these so-called mysteries to inject a bit of excitement into her otherwise uneventful life.

The office doorbell rang.

'That better not be Florence Quail again,' said Connor.

'If it is her, let's hope she's brought some of those Venusian cupcakes she made on Monday,' said Ethan, getting up to answer the door. 'They were the business.'

He swung open the door to find not Florence Quail but a middle-aged woman and a glum-looking boy aged about ten standing in the hallway. The boy was carrying a large cardboard box labelled **Nutty Choc Blobs** on his shoulder. Ethan's eyes lit up. He liked Nutty Choc Blobs even more than Florence's Venusian cupcakes.

'Are you the Space Detectives?' asked the

woman. She had a grey, haunted look on her face. 'I need help. Urgently.'

'Come in,' said Ethan. 'I think we can spare you a few minutes.'

The woman introduced herself as Mrs Marjorie Plum and the boy as her son Felix. Ethan showed them into the office and asked them to sit on the long, comfortable sofa facing the two detectives' desks. He expected Felix to put down the cardboard box – hoping he would open it and offer its contents around – but to his surprise the boy kept the box held firmly on his shoulder. It looked very uncomfortable.

'I'm Connor,' said Connor, 'and that's Ethan. We solve problems. What can we do for you?'

Mrs Plum took a deep, shuddering breath. She seemed to be gathering herself to deliver some shocking revelation. 'It's probably easier if we show you,' she said, and nodded at Felix, giving his arm a gentle nudge.

'I'll show you, guys,' said Felix morosely, 'but you've got to promise to be cool about this and not freak out.'

Connor and Ethan exchanged a curious glance.

'We promise,' said Connor.

'We'll be cool,' said Ethan.

'OK,' said Felix, 'but remember. You promised.'

He lifted the Nutty Choc Blobs box from his shoulder and placed it on the floor.

Connor and Ethan blinked. Then blinked again. Then rubbed their eyes and blinked some more.

It must be extremely difficult to be cool and not freak out when a boy reveals an extra head sprouting from his shirt collar, but a promise is a promise and somehow Connor and Ethan managed it. They stared as politely as possible and tried their hardest not to say things like *wow* and *oh my gosh* and *blinking heck, mate, you've got two heads!*

Mark Powers has been making up ridiculous stories since primary school. He grew up in North Wales and now lives in Manchester. If he could go anywhere in space he'd like to go to the Planet of the Doughnuts (that is a thing, isn't it?)

Dapo Adeola is a total sci-fi enthusiast who loves creating characters for books and animation. He grew up in South London and now resides in East London, which according to him is about as close to another world as you're gonna get here on earth.

LOOK OUT FOR

Dan is a teddy bear.
He's made for hugging.
Aw, so cute, right?

WRONG!

Dan's so strong he can CRUSH CARS.
But what makes him a FAULTY TOY
could make him the PERFECT SPY.

With a robot police rabbit
and one seriously angry doll, Dan is in
a **TOP SECRET TEAM** designed to
STOP CRIMINALS in their tracks.

It's all up to the

SPY TOYS!